Bobby Brewster's wishbone

H. E. TODD

Illustrated by Lilian Buchanan

HODDER & STOUGHTON
LONDON LEICESTER SYDNEY AUCKLAND

ISBN 0 340 21400 7

Text copyright © 1974 H. E. Todd
Illustrations copyright © 1974 Hodder & Stoughton Ltd
First published in 1974 by Brockhampton Press Ltd
(now Hodder & Stoughton Children's Books)
Second edition 1977
Filmset by Keyspools Ltd, Golborne, Lancs.
Printed Offset Litho in Great Britain, for Hodder & Stoughton
Children's Books, a division of Hodder & Stoughton Ltd,
Arlen House, Salisbury Road, Leicester, by
Cox & Wyman Ltd, London, Fakenham and Reading

Contents

A happy wishbone

Cars are very useful things to own, but they can be a nuisance when they go wrong, especially in the middle of a journey and miles from anywhere. And I'm afraid that Mr Brewster – that's Bobby's father – isn't much good at putting them right when they *do* go wrong.

Mind you, Mr Brewster is a good safe driver, which is a very good thing because he has to drive many thousands of miles a year on business. In fact he drives so far that his cars usually have to be changed at the end of each year. I say 'usually' because there has been one exception, and that is the car he owns at present. He has already kept this for over two years, and driven it thousands and thousands of miles. It never lets him down, and is such a comfortable and friendly car that everyone in the family is fond of it. They affectionately call it 'Charley'.

Mr Brewster is so fond of his car that he started saying 'Good morning' and 'Thank you' to it, and when Bobby heard his father do this one evening he thought that he would try it as well. So on the very next morning he quietly slipped out to the garage, sat in the driver's seat, patted the steering wheel, and said loudly, 'Good morning, Charley.'

Then a very funny thing happened.

'Good morning, Bobby,' replied a voice, and he thought that it could only have come from the car because there was no one else there.

'I didn't know you could talk, Charley,' said Bobby, but there was no reply so he still wasn't sure that he had really heard anything.

That afternoon he was taken for a drive, and when they parked in the garage his father, as usual, patted Charley and thanked him before getting out. There was no reply, but Bobby stayed in the car and pretended to be looking for something, and then *he* patted it and said, 'Good night, Charley, and thank you.'

Then another funny thing happened.

The voice replied, 'Good night, Bobby, and thank you too' – but that was all. Bobby tried to continue the conversation but the voice would say no more. And for several weeks it continued to reply to Bobby's greetings – but never any more than that, and never when anyone else was there.

Well, that was all fairly exciting, wasn't it? It was certainly Bobby Brewster magic, but not much use to anybody. After all, if *people* you know just say 'Good morning' and 'Good night' but nothing else, they're not very interesting, are they?

But then, one morning, the first useful magic happened. Bobby slipped out to the garage to say his usual 'Good morning,

Charley', and the voice answered with the single word:

'Tyre.'

Then, when Bobby inspected the tyres, he noticed that one of them was rather flat. So he warned his father about it, who was most thankful and congratulated him on being so observant.

'Ha,' thought Bobby, 'now perhaps we're getting somewhere.'

'No he doesn't,' said his father.

'Are you *sure*?' asked Bobby, rather surprised.

'Positive,' answered his father. 'The pressure gauge is right up to normal' – and he drove on.

After a short time Bobby felt worried, so he persisted. 'Father, I *still* think Charley needs some oil.'

'Why?' demanded his father.

Bobby couldn't very well say, 'Because he asked for it.' He said rather lamely, 'I just think so, that's all,' and his father snorted and drove on.

A few minutes later Bobby could contain himself no longer and he urged, 'Father, *please* give Charley some oil.'

'I've told you, he doesn't need any oil,' snapped his father.

'I'm *sure* he does,' cried Bobby frantically. 'Please *do* stop at the next garage.'

Then Mrs Brewster added her plea.

'For heaven's sake, do as Bobby asks, Henry,'

she said. 'You can always fill up with petrol, and if you don't satisfy him now we shall have nothing but oil for the rest of the day.'

'Oh, all right,' said Bobby's father reluctantly. He drew in at the next garage, and after being served with petrol he casually said to the attendant, 'I don't think I need any, but please check my oil, will you?'

'Certainly, sir,' said the attendant, and when he looked at the dip stick his eyes nearly popped out of his head. He wiped it and tried again, and on inspecting it a second time said, 'My goodness, sir, it's a good thing you checked. You're nearly out of oil.'

'What?' cried Mr Brewster.

'If you had driven much farther, your engine might have seized up,' said the attendant.

'But my pressure gauge is right up,' said Mr Brewster. 'Look at it.'

'Then it must have stuck, sir,' said the attendant. 'While your engine is switched off it should be right down.'

'So it should,' agreed Mr Brewster. 'It's very misleading. I must have it put right.'

'You must indeed,' replied the attendant. 'You should never risk running out of oil.'

Bobby was sensible enough not to say, 'I told you so,' nor was the subject of oil mentioned for the rest of the day. A good time was had by all at the picnic, and Mr Brewster returned home a wiser man.

Charley did not show his real magic again until Christmas Day, which is a very appropriate time for magic. The Brewsters always spend it at home, and there was no need to use a car, but Bobby thought the least he could do was to wish Charley a happy Christmas.

After looking at his presents he went quietly out to the garage and sat in the driving seat.

'A happy Christmas, Charley,' he said.

'Wishbone,' said Charley.

'I beg your pardon?' asked Bobby.

'*Wishbone,*' repeated Charley.

'He must be thinking of turkey,' thought

Bobby. 'And what a novel way of answering a Christmas greeting.' So for the rest of the day, whenever anyone wished him 'A happy Christmas', he replied, 'A happy wishbone' – and everybody laughed, Bobby himself loudest of all. At dinner time his mother allowed him to pull the turkey wishbone with her, but I'm afraid that she pulled the longer piece, so he didn't get a wish.

Christmas Day passed all too quickly, as it usually does, but on the following morning Bobby still felt in a festive mood, so he went out to the garage and wished Charley 'A happy Boxing Day'.

'*Wishbone,*' said Charley.

'I beg your pardon?' asked Bobby Brewster.

'*Wishbone,*' repeated Charley – but that was all he would say.

This made Bobby laugh, and he soon had wishbones on the brain. The Brewsters went to their usual Boxing Day party, and he spent most of the time wishing everybody 'a happy

'Don't be ridiculous, Bobby,' snapped his father, who was thoroughly fed up with wishbones.

'He's not being ridiculous, Mr Brewster,' said the garage man. 'Do you know, I think he might be right.'

'Right about what?' asked Mr Brewster.

'The knocking *could* be due to trouble with the wishbone. It's a good thing Bobby suggested it. It could save a lot of time,' said the garage man. 'If you will just leave it with me for an hour or two, I will look, and put it right.'

So they did – and Bobby *was* right. I won't go into technical details, but I'm told that under the front of some cars there is a metal thing called a wishbone which has something to do with the shock absorbers. Fitted to the wishbone, to stop it knocking against other metal, is a rebound rubber, and poor old Charley's rebound rubber had worn, so he was having trouble with a knocking wishbone

– which must be a very uncomfortable thing to have.

So, you see, all the time Bobby had been sickening his parents with wishbones, he wasn't being nearly as silly as he sounded. Without knowing it himself, he was almost telling the truth. But to tell the complete truth about Charley he really should have been repeating, 'An *unhappy* wishbone.'

And that would have sounded sillier still and irritated his parents even more!

The milkman's horse

Bobby Brewster gets on very well with all the tradesmen and people who call regularly at the house. There's the paperboy and the postman and the baker's boy and the greengrocer. But best of all he likes the milkman. For two reasons. Firstly, although the milkman is an elderly gentleman with white hair, he always calls Bobby 'Mr Brewster', which makes him feel rather important. Secondly, the milkman has a horse. You don't often see horses pulling milkcarts now, but Bobby Brewster's milkman has a horse. Not an ordinary horse, oh dear me, no. Like the milkman, the horse is elderly. Also like the milkman, it has some white hairs. In fact, it's quite like the milkman in many ways except that the horse sometimes

23

wears blinkers and the milkman never does. It's a very well-behaved horse and never begs for sugar, although it is pleased to accept some if it is offered. But although it's quite a big animal, it's such a gentle creature that Bobby really loves it. And I'm sure you would, too, if you could meet it.

Well, one Friday, the morning for paying bills, there was a ring at the back door and Bobby answered it. There stood the milkman, rather out of breath.

'Good morning, Mr Brewster,' he said, panting rather heavily.

At that moment Bobby's mother came to the back door.

'Good morning,' she said. 'You don't look very well.'

'I'm afraid I don't feel very well,' said the milkman.

'What's the matter?' asked Mrs Brewster.

'I've got a pain in my stomach and I'm very short of breath,' said the milkman.

'You'd better come inside and sit down,' said Mrs Brewster. 'We can't have you breaking down in the middle of your round.'

And when Mrs Brewster asked him what he would like to drink, do you know what he asked for? A glass of milk.

In the meantime Bobby thought he had better go and see how the milkman's horse was getting on. It was quite happy eating grass from the verge by the front gate. But when Bobby arrived, a very funny thing happened. The horse raised its head, looked straight at Bobby and winked, a great big wink with the left eye. Well, of course Bobby winked back.

'Good,' said the horse, 'so you can wink as well.'

'Certainly I can,' said Bobby, 'and I'm jolly glad now to have a talk to you. Do you feel all right?'

'Yes,' said the horse. 'Why? Don't I look well?'

'Perfectly,' said Bobby, 'but your milkman isn't. He's sitting in our kitchen with a stomach ache, drinking a glass of milk.'

'Poor old Clarence,' said the horse. 'I thought he seemed a bit short of breath this morning. I've never known him out of sorts before.'

'I don't know when he'll be able to finish his round,' said Bobby. 'I think he needs a rest, you know. I wish we could help him.'

'Jolly good idea,' said the horse. 'We will.'

'We will do what?' asked Bobby.

'We'll finish his round for him,' said the horse.

'How can we?' asked Bobby. 'I don't know the way.'

'I do,' said the horse.

'And I don't know the names of any of the people or how much milk they want,' said Bobby.

'My dear boy,' said the horse, 'do you think I've been tramping round these streets for years and years without learning a thing or two? I know the name of every man, woman and child on the company's books, and how much milk they take. And if you really wanted to know, I believe I could tell you all their sizes in socks.'

'I do beg your pardon,' said Bobby. 'I didn't realize that you were such a clever horse.'

'Oh, that's quite all right,' said the horse. 'You couldn't possibly be expected to know.

Come on now, get hold of the reins and we'll get on with the round.'

The first stop was at number 14.

'Three pints for Mrs Batchelor,' said the horse, 'and if she comes to the door please ask her from me how her son, Bertie, is getting on at school.'

Bobby carefully carried three pints to the door, and Mrs Batchelor was waiting outside.

'Hello,' she said, 'you're not our usual milk-man.'

'No,' said Bobby, 'I'm afraid he's got a stomach ache and he's very short of breath.'

'Oh, I *am* sorry,' said Mrs Batchelor. 'How did you know what milk I wanted?'

'The horse told me,' said Bobby.

'I beg your pardon?' asked Mrs Batchelor.

'I said the horse told me,' said Bobby, 'and he also told me to ask you how Bertie Batchelor is getting on at school. He's a very clever horse.'

'He must be,' said Mrs Batchelor, 'and you can tell your very clever horse from me that Bertie is enjoying school very much and he's top of the class.'

'That's good,' said Bobby, 'I will.'

So he did, and the horse was delighted. Well, they got on famously with the round. That horse really did know everybody's name and how much milk they needed. He even knew that the Joneses wanted an extra pint

29

because Jimmy was getting over the measles and needed building up. Mrs Jones was most impressed and said that she would write to the milk company to congratulate them on their very clever horse and milkboy.

There was one awkward moment. Outside one of the last houses the horse said, 'I should leave that one pint very quietly and come away quickly. A grumpy-looking man with a beard lives here.'

Bobby felt rather frightened when he found the man waiting for him at the door. But he needn't have worried. The man said, 'You're a very nice boy, and you've got a very nice horse. Please give him this lump of sugar with my compliments.'

And when the horse was eating it afterwards it said, 'Well, that goes to prove that you can't tell from appearances, doesn't it?'

They finished the round quite quickly and the horse said, 'Hold your arm out to warn the traffic, and home we go.'

So they turned round and went back to the Brewsters' house. When Bobby ran inside, the milkman was just finishing his milk.

'Well,' he said to Mrs Brewster, 'I don't feel like it, but I'm afraid I must go and finish my round.'

'There's no need to,' said Bobby, 'it's finished.'

'I beg your pardon?' asked the milkman.

'I said your round's finished,' said Bobby.

'Who by?' asked the milkman.

'Your horse and me,' said Bobby.

The milkman was very agitated. He was afraid they had gone to all the wrong places. But he needn't have worried. When he enquired he found that all the milk had been delivered perfectly and that not a single bottle had been broken.

'How did you know how much milk to leave?' he asked Bobby.

'Your horse told me,' said Bobby.

'I beg your pardon?' said the milkman.

'I said, your horse told me,' said Bobby. 'And what's more he told me that your name is Clarence.'

'Well, I always knew that Harry was the cleverest horse in the world,' said the milkman, 'but I never knew he could talk before.'

'He can only talk to me,' said Bobby.

'Why?' asked the milkman.

'Ah,' said Bobby, 'that's a secret, and I'm afraid I can't tell you.'

And do you know, from that day to this, whenever Bobby is at home he goes and whispers in the horse's ear, and whilst the horse whispers back the milkman stands and looks and scratches his head.

Garters

I don't want to be critical, but I have to admit that there have been times when Bobby Brewster has looked very scruffy. Not that he liked being untidy, but it just seemed to happen to him that way. Some boys are like that, and he was definitely one of them.

To start with, there was the hair. When it had been well brushed for church, it looked very nice, but church only happens occasionally, and for the rest of the week the hairbrush was used all too little. Round the neck – or more or less round it – was a grey and red striped school tie. Why is it that ties stay properly tied for some people but not for others? Bobby was one of the others.

Then, moving further down, we come to the problem of the flapping shirt. Now when playing games – and indeed most of the time – Bobby was keen and vigorous, with the result that his shirt became untucked, and flapped out at the back, allowing his trousers to hang lower than they ought. And talking about things hanging lower than they ought, what about his stockings? Sometimes they didn't even hang at all. They just flapped round his ankles, usually over very muddy shoes.

But recently there have been signs of improvement in Bobby Brewster's appearance. Mrs Brewster secretly prides herself that this is the result of her complaints, but as a matter of fact she is wrong. It all started when a very funny thing happened to his stockings. At least, not exactly to his stockings, but to the things that try to keep them up. His garters.

Do you wear garters? Bobby Brewster does though he first put them on much against his will. When he started school they weren't necessary. His smart grey school stockings, with the red stripe round the turnover, were elasticated at the knee and stayed up by themselves. But sooner or later elastic loses its strength, and in Bobby's case it was sooner because he was always in such a rush when he dressed and undressed that he pulled his stockings on and off far too roughly. So day by day they dropped lower and lower till his mother said at last, 'Bobby, I really *must* make you a pair of garters.'

'Why?' demanded Bobby, rather rudely.

'To keep your stockings up, of course,' replied his mother. 'They look ridiculous flapping round your ankles like that.'

'Lots of boys wear them that way,' protested Bobby.

'What lots of boys do is their affair,' said his mother. 'I'm certainly not sending you to school like that. I shall buy some elastic today.'

So she did, three-quarters of a yard of white elastic, half an inch wide, at 4p a yard. So you can work out for yourself how much that cost, can't you?

At first Bobby resented wearing his new garters. For one thing they felt tight, and when he took off his stockings there was a red ridge below his knees showing the pattern of the knitting. Besides, he felt conspicuous because he was one of the few boys at school whose stockings always stayed up.

But then he found that there was an advantage. He discovered this one evening at bed-time, when a garter fell out of his stockings. He opened it with his fingers to see how wide it would stretch when it suddenly slipped off and shot across the bedroom.

'That's fun,' he thought. So he tried it again, and it worked. Then he started aiming at things, including a fly on the wall. For the next half hour that poor fly had a miserable time because whenever it settled anywhere Bobby shot at it with his garter. He always missed, but it was very upsetting for the fly,

expecially as the window was closed and it couldn't escape. Relief came when Bobby stretched the elastic wider than ever and the garter snapped back on his other finger. This made him jump and wring his hand, and the fly chuckled – but Bobby couldn't hear it because flies can only chuckle silently to themselves.

For a time after that Bobby turned into a

real garter pest. At school he would quietly remove both his garters whilst sitting at his desk so that he could shoot them at other boys during play time. Of course they picked them up and shot them back, and once Bobby was hit in the eye with his own garter, which served him right.

Getting Bobby to school every morning became a perfect nightmare for Mrs Brewster. He could never find his garters when dressing, and the plaintive cry would float down the stairs:

'Mother, where are my garters?'

'Probably on your stockings, dear.'

'I can't find them.'

'Where did you have them last?'

Then Bobby would remember that he had been shooting them about the bedroom before going to bed the night before, and of course it had never occurred to him to find them and put them ready for the morning. So the search on hands and knees would start, and the garters would eventually be found in the most difficult places – under the bed, or behind the wardrobe. All except once, when one garter was completely missing. Later that day his mother found it on the flower bed beneath his bedroom window, where he had shot it without noticing. It had been pouring with rain all day, and the garter was sopping wet, and when Bobby came home from school his mother had a few well-chosen words to say about taking care of clothes.

Well, as you can imagine, all this did the garters no good at all, and I really believe they would soon have become useless. But then, one evening, after he had undressed ready for bed, a very funny thing happened. Bobby screwed up one of his stockings and balanced it on the bedrail for a target. Then he stretched one of his garters and took aim, when a voice cried, 'Stop it!'

'I beg your pardon?' said Bobby Brewster.

'I said, stop it,' repeated the voice. 'If you

stretch me any more I shall fly backwards and hit you in the eye.'

'Who are you?' asked Bobby.

'I'm your garter,' said the voice. 'I'm magic, and I'm just about fed up with being shot all over the place. And so is my magic brother. We're supposed to be used for keeping up stockings, not shooting at things.'

'I'm very sorry,' said Bobby, 'I thought it was fun.'

'It may be fun for you,' said the garter, 'but it's extremely uncomfortable for us. If you stretch us much more we shall lose our strength and be quite useless. And there's another thing. Can't you make up your mind which leg to put each of us on? You keep chopping and changing. I'm supposed to be a left-handed garter and my brother here is right-handed.'

'How can you be left-*handed* when you only go on my legs?' asked Bobby.

'That's beside the point,' said the garter.

'Anyway,' continued Bobby, 'you both look exactly alike, and I'm sure my mother didn't think about special legs when she made you in the first place. She just made two garters. How do you know which leg you're each supposed to fit?'

'We will show you in a minute if you behave,' replied the garter. 'But first you must make some promises. Firstly, you must promise never to shoot us without good reason. Twice a day is quite enough – once when you get up, and once at bed time.'

'It sounds like taking medicine,' said Bobby.

'It *is* like taking medicine in a way,' agreed the garter. 'Magic medicine to make you sensible and tidy.'

'Can I show your magic to anyone else?' asked Bobby.

'No,' said the garter. 'It's magic only for you. It won't work for anyone else. But before we show it to you, what about those promises? You must never shoot us except at morning and night, and also you must always keep your stockings up, your shirt tucked in, your tie straight, and your hair brushed.'

'Always?' asked Bobby doubtfully.

'Well, nearly always, anyway,' replied the garter.

'Won't you show me your magic first, to see how good it is?' asked Bobby. 'They seem such very difficult promises to keep.'

'No,' said the garter firmly. 'The promises must be made first.'

'Oh, very well then,' said Bobby reluctantly. 'I only hope it's worth it.'

'Right,' said the garter. 'Now aim me at the window and shoot me.'

'Hard?' asked Bobby.

'As hard as you like,' said the garter.

Bobby took careful aim, stretched the elastic as far as he could, and fired. The garter flew straight towards the window, then turned back in a graceful left-handed circle, and landed back on the chair by his side. It did, really.

'My word,' cried Bobby. 'That was good.'

'Now fire my brother,' said the garter on the chair.

So Bobby did, and it flew in a beautiful right-handed circle and also landed on the chair.

'That's marvellous,' cried Bobby. 'Just like a boomerang. Can I do it again?'

'Not tonight,' said the garter. 'Remember what I said. Once at bed time, and once in the morning. Wait till tomorrow when you get up. Then we will each fly straight back into your hand. I will always fly in a left-handed circle, and my brother in a right-handed circle. So you will know which leg to put us on, won't you? Is that magic enough for you?'

'Indeed it is,' cried Bobby. 'And I promise to keep my promises.'

And he has. Of course, the magic makes it easier for him. Every morning his garters show him which leg they fit by flying straight back to his hand in different circles, and every evening they shoot back onto the chair with his other clothes, ready for the morning, so they are never lost. And from that day to this his stockings always stay up to show the smart red stripe round the turnover. That makes him feel that his legs are so smart that the least he can do is keep the rest of himself smart by tucking his shirt in, keeping his tie straight, and usually, but not quite always, brushing his hair.

So everyone is far happier than they were. Mrs Brewster, Bobby himself, his garters – and that fly, if it's still alive.

The lift

When Mrs Brewster has important shopping to do, she sometimes goes to a large store in a town several miles away. The store is called Hardcastle's, and she enjoys shopping there because everybody is so friendly. Bobby enjoys shopping there too. Not that he ever buys much, but he has made several friends, and he talks to them while his mother choses clothes, because listening to ladies chosing clothes is very boring and takes a long time. Once or twice Bobby has even talked to Mr Hardcastle himself, the owner of the store.

But Bobby's greatest friend in that store is Fred Harris the liftman. The regular customers just call him Fred, but Bobby calls him Mr Harris, which is only right and proper. They first met when Bobby was quite young and travelling on a lift for the first time. Later, when they made another visit, Fred said to Bobby's mother, 'Leave Bobby here with me, madam, while you do your shopping. I'll look after him for you.' Mrs Brewster thought that was a splendid idea. She was going to buy a hat for a wedding, and didn't want to be rushed.

So Fred has looked after Bobby ever since then. At least, every visit except one, and you'll find out what I mean by that when you read this story.

Bobby always had a grand time on that lift. Firstly, it gave him a funny feeling in his tummy when it went up and down, and once he got used to it the feeling was quite exciting. Then Fred Harris was so cheerful with everybody. He knew a great many customers by name and greeted them like old friends, which they were. And he made his announcement on each floor in a most impressive voice, like this:

department doing up parcels.'

'Why?' asked Bobby.

'They're going to turn this into an automatic lift' said Fred. 'One that goes up and down on it's own and announces the floors itself.'

'How could it possibly do that?' asked Bobby.

'I don't know how it does it, but that's what they say it's going to do,' said Fred. 'All I *do* know is that I'm going to miss my old lift.'

And he patted the lever affectionately, almost with tears in his eyes.

'It's a shame,' said Bobby. 'I'm going to miss you, and so are lots of other customers. We don't want any silly old automatic lift.'

By the time of their next visit some months later, there were great alterations in Hardcastle's store. It all looked very shiny and impressive, but somehow not so homely. And as for the lift, it was a vision in aluminium and glass with an indicator above it that lit up.

When Bobby first saw it the light said 'LIFT GOING UP', and then, when the lift glided from the basement to the ground floor, a hissing voice announced: 'Ground floor. Haberdashery, cosmetics, jewellery, hosiery and gloves. Please stand clear of the gates.' Bobby stared in amazement as some customers left the lift and he stepped inside with his mother. Then the hissing voice said, 'Stand clear of the gates please. Going up', and up they glided to the first floor, where the hissing voice made its announcement, the doors slid open, and out they went.

That was all very exciting, wasn't it? But somehow Bobby couldn't help saying to himself, as he walked with his mother to the dress department, 'Oh dear, I *do* miss Mr Harris the liftman.' Certainly the automatic lift took people up and down very well, and never left a step for them to trip over, but it wasn't nearly so friendly.

While his mother was in the dress department he thought he would slip back and ride up and down to all the floors. At first everything went well, with the lift running smoothly and announcing everything correctly, except that several customers looked round with a disappointed expression as they entered and said 'Where's Fred?'

Then a funny thing happened – or rather, lots of funny things started happening. First of all the lift voice announced on the second floor that it was 'going up' and promptly started to 'go down'. Then, when it reached the first floor it announced: 'Third floor. Carpets and soft furnishings. Please stand clear of the gates', and several customers got off to buy carpets and found they were in the ladies' clothing department. They rushed back into the lift as it was announcing 'going down', and it shot straight up to the fourth floor without stopping and announced, 'Second floor. Toys, hardware and china. Please stand clear of the gates.'

As you can imagine, there was great confusion. Nobody knew which floor they were really on or which departments were on which floor. Then the voice went quite mad. Instead of announcing 'going up' or 'going down', it started saying ridiculous things like 'going forwards', 'going backwards' and even 'going sideways'! Then, as it stopped on each floor, it announced all sorts of absurd departments like, 'First floor. Footballs, fruit and fish forks.' And, 'Second floor. Suit cases, sausages and sardine sandwiches.'

But the final straw came when the voice started making remarks about the customers.

'Stand clear of the gates, please, and will that lady in the silly red hat please stop pushing.'

'Stand clear of the gates please. And I must ask the very stout gentleman with the bald head to get off the lift, or we shall never reach the top.'

Well, by this time not only were all the customers completely confused, but some of them were very annoyed, so Bobby thought he had better find Mr Hardcastle, the owner of the store, and tell him what was happening.

'Mr Hardcastle,' he said, 'something seems to have gone wrong with your new lift.'

'What's the matter with it?' asked Mr Hardcastle.

'I think you had better come and see for yourself,' said Bobby. 'If I told you you'd never believe me.'

So Mr Hardcastle and Bobby hurried to the

lift and arrived just as it was announcing:

'Ground floor. Not going up or down. If you want to go anywhere use the stairs because I'm tired.'

'Be careful what you're saying, my man,' started Mr Hardcastle indignantly – and then he stopped when he realized there wasn't a man there. Just a voice. He and Bobby stepped into the empty lift and the door closed immediately as the voice said, 'Stand clear of the gates please. Going up.'

Half way between the first and second floor it suddenly stopped, and there they were, stuck fast.

'What's wrong now?' demanded Mr Hardcastle.

'You are,' said the lift voice.

'I beg your pardon?' asked Mr Hardcastle.

'I said you're wrong,' repeated the lift voice.

'Well, that's a fine thing, I must say,' said Mr Hardcastle. 'After all the trouble you've been causing! What have *I* done wrong?'

'You've got rid of Fred,' accused the lift voice.

'Fred who?' asked Mr Hardcastle.

'Fred Harris, the liftman' said the voice.

'I haven't got rid of him' said Mr Hardcastle. 'He's down in the packing department doing up parcels.'

'That's not the right place for him,' said the voice. 'He ought to be here, in my lift.'

'There's no need for a man in an automatic lift,' said Mr Hardcastle. 'That's the whole point of making it automatic.'

'There's *always* a need for Fred Harris in this lift,' persisted the lift voice. 'He keeps me happy, and he keeps all the customers happy too.'

'Please take me to the next floor at once and allow me to manage my own store,' demanded Mr Hardcastle indignantly.

'Certainly not,' said the lift voice. 'Not until you promise to put Fred Harris back on the lift.'

'I shall do nothing of the sort,' said Mr Hardcastle. 'I shall press your emergency button instead.'

So he did. The lift started to glide upwards, rushed past the second floor before the door could be opened, and stopped dead half-way between the second and third floors.

'What on earth are we going to do now?' asked Mr Hardcastle.

'Nothing at all, I'm afraid,' said Bobby Brewster. 'We're stuck between the second and third floors. And, you know, Mr Hardcastle, it's quite right about Mr Harris. Most of the customers *do* want him back in the lift.'

'We want Fred Harris,' suddenly shouted the lift voice. In fact it shouted so loudly that people waiting on the second and third floors heard, and as most of them agreed they joined in as well:

'We want Fred Harris!'

Their shouts were heard on the first and fourth floors, and soon the whole building, right down to the basement, was ringing with the cry:

'WE WANT FRED HARRIS! WE WANT FRED HARRIS!'

Well, stuck in the lift with all that noise going on, there was only one thing Mr Hardcastle could do to stop it, wasn't there? So he did it.

'Very well,' he said, 'I will put Fred Harris back on the lift.'

Straight away, without another word, or without any button being pressed, the lift glided down to the basement. Fred Harris was already waiting there because he had heard his name being shouted and wondered what it was all about. The door opened and out stepped Mr Hardcastle.

'Fred Harris,' he said, 'you can go back on the lift. But for heaven's sake see that it behaves itself.'

A happy grin spread over Fred's face as he stepped back into his beloved lift.

57

'Thank you, sir,' he said. Then he drew himself up proudly and announced:

'Basement. Toys, hardware and china. Going up. Please stand clear of the gates.'

Bobby went back up to the first floor and hurried anxiously to the dress department in case his mother was wondering what had happened to him. He needn't have worried. Even after all that time she still hadn't quite made up her mind which dress to buy.

Fun in the frost

Do you ever forget something you've been told? Bobby Brewster does and so do his mother and father. Bobby forgets because he doesn't always listen properly to instructions in the first place and they go in one ear and out of the other. Mr and Mrs Brewster forget because the older they get, the more difficult it is to remember.

There are all sorts of ways, of course, to help you to remember things. Bobby Brewster sometimes ties a knot in his handkerchief. That idea works, but it annoys his mother because the knots get very tight to untie and they make his handkerchiefs grubby. Still, it is better than biting holes in his handkerchiefs, which is another habit of his.

But for a brief time early last December the problem of remembering things was solved for Bobby in a magical way. Indeed, it was solved for his mother and father, too, which made it even more magic. It all started on the very first really frosty day of the year. The frost on the ground lay as thick as a coating of snow, and the gaunt trees against the sky made a delicate filigree in white.

Bobby got out of bed later than he ought that morning – he often does on cold, dark days – and was in a rush to get to school. He put on his overcoat and gloves, opened the front door and, as the hall light shone out over the front lawn, he noticed a word clearly written in the frost:

SATCHEL

'My word, I nearly forgot,' he said to himself, and rushed back to fetch it, but he was in so much of a hurry that he was half-way to school before he had time to wonder who had written the word.

'I suppose Mother wrote it,' he thought, 'when she collected the newspaper at the front door, and realized that I was so late that I was sure to forget. It was very clever of her.'

So when he got home from school that afternoon, he said, 'Thank you for reminding me, Mother.'

'Reminding you of what?' asked his mother.

'To take my satchel to school,' said Bobby, 'by writing "Satchel" in the frost on the front lawn this morning. Was the word still there when you went shopping later in the morning?'

'The only word I saw written in the frost was there to remind *me*, not you,' replied Mrs Brewster. 'It was CARRIER BAG.'

'That's funny,' said Bobby.

'Yes, and very useful too,' said his mother, 'because I had completely forgotten it. But the word had disappeared when I returned home. I suppose it must have been frosted over when I was out shopping.'

'That's funnier still,' said Bobby. 'I think something peculiar is happening.'

And when his father came home, there was no doubt about it. Something very peculiar indeed was happening.

'Here's a present for you, Bobby,' said Mr Brewster, handing him a bag of toffees, 'for being such a clever boy and saving me so much money.'

Bobby looked blank.

'How?' he asked.

'It's even colder tonight than last night,' said Mr Brewster, 'and I'm sure the water in my car radiator would have frozen up if you hadn't reminded me by writing ANTI-FREEZE in the frost on the front lawn.'

'But I didn't write it,' cried Bobby.

'Then who did?' asked his father.

'I'm sure I don't know,' said Bobby, 'but it's certainly somebody with a lot of sense. He seems to know what we've forgotten before we know ourselves. What's more, his messages disappear as soon as they're read by the person they're meant for. It must be some of Jack Frost's magic.'

And the next day, which was Saturday, and even colder and whiter, proved to be one full of Jack Frost's fun.

It started when Mrs Wilson called during the morning on Women's Institute business and rubbed her feet vigorously on the mat in the hall saying, 'It was very sensible of you,

Bobby. If I hadn't read your warning, I might have trod white frost all over your mother's sitting-room carpet.'

'What warning?' asked Bobby.

'WIPE YOUR FEET written in frost on the front lawn,' said Mrs Wilson. 'Look.'

So they did, but it wasn't.

'How extraordinary,' said Mrs Wilson, and I agree with her, don't you?

But more extraordinary things were to follow. During the afternoon there was a ring at the front-door bell. Billy Singleton was there, and he immediately announced, apparently for no reason at all, 'She's much better, thank you.'

'Who is?' asked Bobby in surprise.

'My mother,' said Billy.

'I didn't know she was ill,' said Bobby.

'Then why ask?' said Billy.

'I didn't,' said Bobby.

'You did,' said Billy, 'you wrote HOW'S YOUR MOTHER in the frost outside.'

'Show me then,' said Bobby.

But of course Billy couldn't.

'Never mind,' said Bobby, 'I'm glad your mother's better anyway,' which left Billy Singleton looking completely mystified.

The last and funniest incident of all was just before tea, and Bobby saw it all. His father was horrified to see Mr Bompass opening the garden gate. Mr Bompass is not popular in the Brewster household. In fact, he's one of the few people in the district who they really dislike. They think he is both bad-tempered and too pleased with himself.

'Oh dear,' groaned Mr Brewster, 'I suppose he's come to complain about something as usual.'

And he had. As soon as he was ushered into the sitting-room he started moaning about something. Mr Brewster tried to pacify him, but it was useless, and in the end Mr Bompass was still dissatisfied and stalked out of the front door, slamming it rudely behind him.

In the kitchen Mrs Brewster sighed with relief. 'He's gone,' she said. And at that very moment Bobby, who was looking out of the window, was amazed to see the words GOOD RIDDANCE clearly printed in the frost on the lawn. Mr Bompass saw them too. He went very red in the face, snorted and strode angrily away. As he disappeared out of the front gate, the words disappeared on the front lawn, but he never called on the Brewsters again, not even to complain.

opened them on Christmas morning, he felt too ill to bother about them much and later they turned out to be more useful than exciting. You know what I mean by that, don't you? Things to wear rather than play with. Of course he thanked everyone and didn't say anything about being disappointed. But there was no doubt that that Christmas generally was not his best ever.

However, he soon forgot about it and spent a happy spring term at school. And then during the holidays just before Easter a very funny thing happened. He was playing in the garden when he noticed a jackdaw hopping about holding something red in its beak. As he

walked towards it the jackdaw cawed and flew away, and Bobby picked up a little plastic Father Christmas which it had dropped on the lawn. He was a jolly-looking Father Christmas who was still smiling in spite of the fact that there were birds' beak holes in his back, and Bobby ran indoors to the kitchen to show him to his mother.

'Why, Bobby,' she said, 'that's the Father Christmas who disappeared from our Christmas tree on Christmas Eve. We put the tree outside the back door for a few moments before carrying it into the dining-room, and by the time we went back Father Christmas had disappeared. We thought the birds must have taken him.'

'They had,' said Bobby. 'I just saw a jackdaw drop him in the middle of the lawn.'

'What a funny thing,' said Mrs Brewster, and Bobby ran upstairs to look more closely at what he had found. Then another funny thing happened.

'Happy Easter, Bobby,' said Father Christmas.

'I beg your pardon?' asked Bobby.

'I said, Happy Easter,' repeated Father Christmas.

'Thanks very much,' said Bobby. 'It isn't often I'm wished a Happy Easter by Father Christmas.'

'It wouldn't have been much good wishing you a Happy Christmas when you were ill in bed, would it?' replied Father Christmas. 'So I thought that as it was snowing and miserable I would take the opportunity of spending Christmas with the birds instead and then coming on to you for Easter.'

'That's very thoughtful of you,' said Bobby. 'I felt there was something lacking about last Christmas and it must have been you. What sort of a time did the birds have?'

'Marvellous,' said Father Christmas. 'They said they had never spent such a Christmas in their lives before.'

'What did they have for Christmas dinner?' asked Bobby.

'Worm,' said Father Christmas. 'One of the most succulent worms they had ever tasted.'

'That was all very well for the birds,' said Bobby, 'but it can't have been a very happy Christmas for the worm.'

'Well, what about your turkey?' replied

Father Christmas. 'I know you didn't eat any this year because you were in bed, but your family did, so it can't have been a very happy Christmas for the turkey either, can it?'

'I suppose not,' agreed Bobby, and quickly changed the subject. 'Did the birds have a Christmas party?' he asked.

'Indeed they did,' said Father Christmas. 'As there were so many of them they had it in your garage. Of course, some birds spend their Christmas abroad but all those who stayed behind came to the party and thoroughly enjoyed it.'

'What did they do?' asked Bobby.

'Played games and sang carols,' said Father Christmas. 'They sang beautifully, too, in four parts, but they used different words and instead of "Away in a Manger" they sang "Away in a Bird Bath".'

'What games did they play?' asked Bobby.

'All sorts,' said Father Christmas. 'Chase and He and Hide-and-Seek. By the time they returned to their nests they were tired out.'

'I'm not surprised,' said Bobby. 'And now you mention it I seem to remember hearing a lot of twittering in the garage whilst I was in bed on Christmas evening, and Father did complain about the state of the top of his car when he took it out later in the week. Where have you been staying since Christmas?'

'In several nests,' said Father Christmas, 'with the robins, the sparrows, the bluetits, the crows, and I have just spent a week with the jackdaw family. They were very kind to me, and I have had a lovely rest since all my work before and during Christmas.'

'The jackdaws must be sorry to lose you,' said Bobby.

'I suppose they are in a way,' agreed Father Christmas, 'but they knew it was only fair for you to have me for Easter, and before I left I made arrangements for them to have a very exciting Easter present. Then Mr Jackdaw gave me a lift to your garden.'

he said to the company in general, 'Do you know, everybody, with all my unexpected presents and this lovely party, it seems just like having Christmas at Easter.'

That's not quite the end of the story. Do you remember that Father Christmas said he had made arrangements for the jackdaws to have a surprise at Easter? Well, so they did. While the Brewsters were eating the chickens for dinner, Mrs Jackdaw was laying three eggs, and when she and her husband looked proudly at them they had the surprise of their lives because all three eggs were covered in silver paper.

Johnny Window

The windows of Hardcastle's store, in the town a few miles from Bobby Brewster's home, are always worth looking at. So many fascinating things are displayed in them, from tea-trays to train sets, and from clocks to clothes. The clothes are shown off by models, and Bobby Brewster thinks the models of grown-up ladies are very odd indeed. They stand in the most ridiculous attitudes in what is supposed to be a smart, sophisticated way, and they all have haughty expressions on their faces.

But the model that shows off the boys' clothes is quite different. He is very life-like, and looks about Bobby's age. Bobby calls him Johnny Window because he always stands in the window looking such a cheerful Johnny. Johnny has a snub nose and a cheeky expression on his face whatever he's wearing. In his pyjamas he looks just as if he's ready for a jolly good pillow-fight, and he doesn't even seem embarrassed when he has to stand in the window all day wearing nothing but a vest and pants.

Bobby makes a point of going to see Johnny Window when he is in the town, not only because he likes the look of him, but for another very special reason. You see, whenever Bobby arrives at Hardcastle's, Johnny Window winks at him. He does, really. A great big wink with the left eye. You probably think that Bobby just imagines it – indeed Bobby thought so himself at first – but one day a very funny thing happened.

It was during Hardcastle's 'sports week' and everything in their window was based on a winter sport. One of the superior young ladies was dressed for hockey, and you could see from the way she was holding her stick that she had never hit a hockey ball in her life. The other was in a skiing outfit, and Bobby thought how dearly he would love to see her fall bonk on her bottom in the snow. But Johnny Window took pride of place, standing on a pedestal that took him round and round and round. He was in football kit, dazzling blue-and-white striped shirt and stockings, white shorts, and shiny black boots with white laces. You could tell just to look at him that he was jolly good at football, and Bobby stood there enthralled.

Then, as the pedestal brought Johnny and Bobby face to face, what do you think Johnny did? He winked. A great big wink with the left eye. He did, really. Bobby was not convinced that he was seeing right, but then, as the pedestal brought Johnny round to face him again, there was another wink. And so it went on, five times in a row. Wink – wink – wink – wink – wink. Well, that proved it,

didn't it? Bobby didn't wait any longer because watching Johnny going round and
round and round on a pedestal made him feel
giddy. Indeed, he began to feel rather sorry for
Johnny, who must surely be getting giddy
himself going round and round and round all
day. But Johnny didn't seem to mind. He
looked just as cheeky as ever whichever way
he was facing.

Now, it so happened that on the following Wednesday afternoon Bobby was due to play in a championship football match. His school under-10s had reached the final of the local competition, and Bobby was very proud to be selected for such an important match. It was an away game against a school in the same town as Hardcastle's store, and Mr Limcano drove the boys there in a minibus. Bobby had butterflies in his tummy as he was changing into football kit, but when he looked at all his team-mates in their bright red shirts and stockings and realised that he must be just as smart as they were, he gained more confidence.

They ran on to the ground together, kicking the football to each other in a way they hoped would look confident, but then Bobby caught sight of the other team and his heart sank. He had never seen more likely looking players. They were dressed in dazzling blue-and-white striped shirts and stockings and white shorts, and they looked to Bobby to be far larger than his own team, and seemed to be running about faster and kicking the ball harder. Of course, that may have been his imagination again. The other team often looks much more impressive before a game than during it, doesn't it? But then Bobby's imagination ran riot – or was it imagination? One of the boys in blue and white stripes was even better than the others. Bobby watched him fascinated as he weaved in and out dribbling the ball before kicking it – wham – into the net.

'Good shot, Johnny,' cried his mates, and when the boy turned round Bobby had the shock of his life. He looked exactly like Johnny Window, and with the same cheeky expression. Bobby stared even harder. Yes, there was no doubt about it, and when the boy saw Bobby staring at him, do you know what he did? He winked. He did, really. A great big wink with the left eye.

Then the game started – and what a game it was! Both teams were on their best form, and the spectators – parents, teachers and children – became more and more excited as it went on.

The other side scored first, through a perfectly placed pass by Johnny to the centre forward. Bobby knew he really was called Johnny because the spectators kept shouting, 'Pass it to Johnny'. Then, before half-time Bobby's side equalized with a splendid goal, and Mr Limcano ran on to the pitch during the interval, while they were sucking their lemons, to give instructions for the second half.

And one of the tips he gave was, 'Be sure to mark the boy they call Johnny very closely, he's good.'

At the beginning of the second half it was clear that the advice had been taken to heart. Bobby's team surged forward into the attack, and Bobby was very proud to give the pass that resulted in another goal. 2–1. They were in the lead. Then play became fast and furious – but never too furious. It's a funny thing that when grown-up men play football, they often lose their tempers and argue with the referee and generally behave like spoiled children. But boys at football usually play for the fun of it and behave as grown-up men ought to behave. That's how this game was played – hard and enthusiastic but never bad-tempered. Indeed, whenever a player was brought down hard by a tackle, he was helped to his feet by the opponent with smiles on both sides. And no one ever appealed to the ref or argued when he made a mistake, which he sometimes did.

Well, time was getting nearer, and it really began to look as if Bobby's team would win the cup. But then the other side equalized with a fine goal. Two all, with five minutes to go. And a few minutes later Johnny was unmarked for once. He dribbled the ball through the opposition – first this way, then that – side-stepped the full back and then drove it into the net with a shot that gave the goalkeeper no chance. Almost immediately the whistle went for time, and Bobby's team had lost.

Of course, they were disappointed, but they smiled quite cheerfully as they lined up for the presentation, and in their heart of hearts thought that the better side had won. The cup was presented amid much clapping and many cheers, and each member of the winning team was handed a large red rosette with the words 'Cup Winners' printed on the button in the middle. Very smart they looked too, when pinned on the chests of their dazzling blue-and-white striped shirts.

A day or two later Bobby was shopping with his mother, and they went to Hardcastle's as they often do. As usual, Bobby made a point of gazing in the window where the sports clothes were still being displayed. There was Johnny Window, revolving on his pedestal, dressed in dazzling blue-and-white football kit, and I am sure there's no need to tell you what he did when he turned round to face Bobby, so I won't. But for once Bobby wasn't looking at Johnny's face. His eyes were pinned on Johnny's chest – where something else was also pinned. Can you guess what it was?

A large red rosette with the words 'Cup Winners' printed on the button in the middle. Wasn't that a coincidence? Or was it?

Further adventures of Bobby Brewster

BOBBY BREWSTER

BOBBY BREWSTER – BUS CONDUCTOR

BOBBY BREWSTER'S SHADOW

BOBBY BREWSTER'S BICYCLE

BOBBY BREWSTER'S CAMERA

BOBBY BREWSTER'S WALLPAPER

BOBBY BREWSTER'S CONKER

BOBBY BREWSTER – DETECTIVE

BOBBY BREWSTER'S POTATO

BOBBY BREWSTER AND THE GHOST

BOBBY BREWSTER'S SCARECROW

BOBBY BREWSTER'S KITE

BOBBY BREWSTER'S TORCH

BOBBY BREWSTER'S BALLOON RACE

BOBBY BREWSTER'S TYPEWRITER

BOBBY BREWSTER'S BEE

BOBBY BREWSTER'S BOOKMARK